What I Shouldn't Say

What I Shouldn't Say

David Asbery & Seymour Swan

Writer's Showcase
presented by *Writer's Digest*
San Jose New York Lincoln Shanghai

What I Shouldn't Say

Writer's Showcase
presented by *Writer's Digest*
an imprint of iUniverse.com, Inc.

For information address:
iUniverse.com, Inc.
5220 S 16th, Ste. 200
Lincoln, NE 68512
www.iuniverse.com

ISBN: 0-595-13281-2

Printed in the United States of America

David's Dedication

To My Mother and My Father

Hattie and Harry Asbery

"Thanks for giving me the best childhood that a boy could ask for."

AND

To My Sons

David and Jamarl

"Daddy followed his dreams. Now you follow yours."

Seymour's Dedication

To My Mother and My Father

Attie and Sidney Swan

"Thanks for your love and support. I love you more than words can tell."

AND

To My Kids

Corey, Jasmine, & Jaylen

"I live for your happiness."

Contents

Acknowledgements

DAVID'S SPECIAL THANKS:

Tanisha Thomas: My baby, my love, my editor—Thank you for all of your support and inspiration.

Wayne Dixon: Thanks for making this a reality.

Damon Wayans: Thanks for believing in me and showing me how to make it happen!

Angela and Keith Holmes: Thanks for the love and support.

Maurena Holder: Thanks so much for all of your help.

My Crew at the Firm: Yolanda Jeter, Keith Coles, Alonzo Settles and Sybrandt Davis—Thanks for our support and inspiration.

Seymour Swan: The funniest comedian in NYC (Plug: See Seymour's show every Friday and Saturday night at The NY Comedy Club, New York, NY.)

Dolores Van Scott: My surrogate mother.

Brenda Thomas and Asim Thomas: Thank you for your love and support. It is well appreciated.

New England Patriot Ed Ellis: Thanks for the NFL experience.

Orielle Ellis Hope and Shana: Thanks for your critique.

Jamel Wright and Mark Christian: My life long friends.

Richard DeJesus: Keep the music flowing.

Joseph Asbery: My little brother who has taken the role of big brother because "Big brother wants to write jokes for a living." I love you.

Relando Henry: Thanks for being the first person that I know to buy a copy of "Bootleg."

Andrea Sheriton: Can't wait for your book to come out!

John Morris: Your always in my thoughts.

The Jackson 5: The best R&B group ever. (Can Tito really play the guitar?)

And last, but not definitely least, a Special, Special Thanks to YOU, The Reader.

Live to Laugh

Acknowledgements

SEYMOUR'S SPECIAL THANKS:

Olga Swan: My true love until the end. Thanks for always having my back.

Ester Swan, Toni Swan & Sherry Tucker: My sisters—Thanks for the love.

Dwayne & Sidney Swan: My brothers, my friends—Thanks for your support.

Damon Wayans: Thanks for paving the way and showing me how to keep them laughing.

Al Martin: Thanks for reminding me to always have fun on stage.

David Asbery: Yo, we did it DAWG!

Abreast

I'm glad that Foxy Brown made the decision to stop parading around everywhere butt naked. I was getting tired of seeing her bloated belly in every other magazine promoting her records. She has a song called, "Meet Me at the Hot Spot." I hope that the "Hot Spot" is Jenny Craig. But I can see that she is trying to better her image. At one point it looked like she was advertising pussy. I wish she would call Lil' Kim and school her because I'm really upset with Lil' Kim. Jamarl, my eight-year old son, was watching the MTV Music Awards with me and saw Lil' Kim's exposed left breast. He hasn't been the same since. The boy is obsessed with titties now. He draws pictures of them in school. He stares at his Momma's titties funny and for some reason he always wants to stay at his Aunt Kathy's house. (She has huge breasts). This shit is really starting to bother me. It seems like he's turning into some sort of pervert, just smiling every time he sees a pair of titties. But I guess I shouldn't be too upset. Imagine if Chris Rock walked on stage with his balls hanging out. That would have really drove him nuts.

"Aunt Kathy, I never want to go back home."

Black Women & Anal Sex

Don't ever make the mistake of asking a black woman for anal sex. I asked my girl one time and she let me have it.

Her: "Nigga, you want to put what where?"

Me: "Uhh…"

Her: "Let me break this down to you so that we won't have to ever go there again. Ain't no way that's ever gonna happen. If you ask me, that's just nasty. What you need to do is stop watching all of those perverted movies ya got hidden behind the sofa. But I'll tell you what I'm willing to do. There is a cucumber in the refrigerator. You let me stick that up your ass and I'll do whatever you want."

I looked at my girlfriend and I really felt bad after asking her to do such a thing. She was right. It's immoral and downright nasty. You can bet that I'll never ask her to do something like that again…By the way, does anyone have a clue as to how one would go about getting cucumber seeds out of your ass? It's not for me; it's for a friend of mine.

The Internet

I read an article about the Internet. It said that the FBI is now monitoring the Internet in an effort to catch would-be pedophiles and weirdoes. This made me think about all of the searches I've made on the Web in the past. I will be graduating from college in the year 2001 and when I start looking for a job I don't want some interviewer pulling out a file on me.

Interviewer: "Okay Mr. Asbery, I see you just recently graduated from Hunter College with a 3.5 GPA. That's very good."

Me: "Well, thank you sir."

Interviewer: "And it says here that you were voted president of the Philosophy Club at Hunter. Wow, that's very impressive."

Me: "Yes, thank you."

A secretary walks in with a file labeled "David Asbery Confidential." She hands it to the interviewer.

Interviewer: "Uh, excuse me Mr. Asbery, more good news I suppose…What the hell? What is this shit? It says here that you have a fetish for bald headed white midgets with bubble butts. What the hell is this?"

Me: "What? Where did you get…"

Interviewer: "Nigger, it's all here in your Internet file. It also says that you've been in the drag queen and S&M chat rooms. Get the fuck out of my office you fucking pervert!"

Gangsta Chef

There is a cooking channel on cable television that features a famous New Orleans chef named Emeril Lagasse. He has the personality of Sylvester Stallone's Rocky saying things like "Forget about it!" and "What you talking bout." The people in the audience go crazy. This made me think, *why not have a show featuring a Gangsta Rapper cooking his favorite meal.*

Gangsta Rapper Sy-Quan: "Yo, Yo, thank you for having me on the show. Big ups to my man, Crisco at Rikers. Keep the faith baby. Today I'm gonna share with you the many different ways that one can capitalize off of my favorite animal, "The Pig." Now I'd like to introduce to you my lovely assistant, Tawanda Jones. Tawanda, bring yo big ass on out here girl…Come on ya'll give it up…Tawanda got an ass like a baby elephant…Damn!"

Tawanda brings out a big healthy pig on a leash.

Gangsta Rapper Sy-Quan: "Okay Tawanda, bring the pig over to me…Okay ya'll, what you want to remember while preparing the pig is that it is essential that you have a leash around the pig's neck so that when you jerk it, like so, you get a nice quick clean kill. You see how I just popped his fucking neck? There are two reasons why we do it this way. One, any other method would be cruel and inhumane. And two, we don't want them animal rights mo'fuckers writing letters and shit. Okay, now that the mo'fucker is dead, what I usually do at this point is pray for the pig, you know sort of like what those Jews do to make their mo'fucker food kosher...Will y'all bow ya heads please."

God, please make this pig good to eat. Don't make him too salty on the account that a lot of mo'fuckers got that hypertension, high blood pressure shit...Amen. Oh yeah one more thing, give a shout out to my main man Crisco who got two to five for shit he didn't do. Peace out God.

Gangsta Rapper Sy-Quan: "Okay, back to the show. What we need to do now is drain this bitch. And what that means is that we have to get the blood up on out of him. Tawanda, hand me my gun...Now as you can see, I'm using a 45 magnum, one of the most powerful guns in the world. You can use a .22 or a .38. It really don't matter. What you do is put the gun to the pig's temple and you blow the pig's head off like so. *POW!* Now that that's done you place the gun back on the counter. Remember to put on the safety clip because most accidents happen in the home and I don't want you calling up Sy-Quan blaming me for some mo'fucking mishap yo. Okay, now it's time to drain this bitch. With the pigs head blown off, you hold the pig by its tail and let blood just drain on out but don't let dat shit go down the drain cause we gonna use the shit later so dat the meat can masturbate in...Oh shit, oh shit did I say masturbate? I meant marinate, marinate oh shit, I'm glad we on cable yo, damn. Okay, Tawanda can you pass me a pan for the blood please....? Tawanda, are you there? Did you hear me? Can you please pass me a pan for the blood. Damn! Excuse me ya'll, I got to go see what this ho is doing."

Tawanda's laying on the floor. Evidently the bullet went through the pigs head and into Tawanda's. Sy-Quan walks over to her.

"Oh shit, oh shit, Tawanda you all right? Oh shit, somebody done did a drive-by right here on my mo'fucking show! Tawanda's dead as a mo'-fucker, oh shit! Yo, it must have been them Crenshaw niggas. Yo, I'm sorry ya'll but due to unfortunate circumcisions we gonna have to cancel the rest our show. I got to get my niggas and make a run up to Crenshaw."

Where's My Dog At?

I've been married for ten years. On our seventh year anniversary, my wife and I ended up going to a therapist, which was a waste of money. After three visits, she gave me a bill for $3,000. I said, "Damn, for $3,000 I should have been able to fuck you." The therapist advised us to bring something new into the relationship because we're bored. That next day I went to Circuit City and bought myself a DVD player. I figured this would make me love her. My wife, on the other hand, came home with a dog. A $1,000 dog I might add. One of those Yorkies. I said, "This dog isn't gonna change our relationship."

My wife proved me wrong. We've had the Yorkie for three years and he does everything with us. After dinner, I wipe my mouth, I look down and he's wiping his mouth. In bed, late at night, when you're fighting for a position, he kicks me and I kick him back. But now he's gotten too comfortable with us. Late at night I can't even turn over and make love to my wife anymore. I'm on top of my wife doing my thing and I look behind me and the dog is licking my ass. I looked back at the dog and yelled, "Hey, what the hell are you doing back.........Heeeeeeeeeeey, that doesn't feel too bad, boy." So now when I making love to my wife, I whistle for him. "Come on boy, Kibbles & Bits."

9

Deaf Ears

My Dad went to the doctor to have his colon examined and my mother wanted me to accompany him for support. My mother also wanted me to go with him because Dad is losing his hearing. She wanted me there just in case my dad had any questions about the procedure. I remember the doctor pulling out this big instrument which looked like a whiffle-ball bat. He then proceeded to explain what he would be doing with it.

Doctor: "Okay, Mr. Swan, we will be inserting this into your anus."

My Dad: "Oh you say that this will be painless?"

Me: "No, Dad. He said ANUS not PAINLESS!"

Dad: "Oh, Payless. I know that store. They have great shoes."

Me: "No dad, he said….Oh forget it, just bend over."

My Dad has always been my hero. When I saw that this doctor was about to have his way with my Dad, it cracked me up. As my father bent over, I couldn't help but laugh because I have never seen my Dad's ass before. As he inserted this baseball bat like instrument in my Dad's ass,

I could swear that the doctor looked at me and winked. So needless to say the ride home was long and quiet. I never looked at Dad the same. Since the incident he has gotten so macho but no one seems to listen to him.

Dad: "Seymour, get up off your ass and go to the store for me now!!!"

Me: "You're telling me to get up off my ass? You should have told that doctor to get up off yours…!"

The New Black Man

I'm proud to announce that Black men are now eating pussy. They're no longer avoiding it like it's pork. No more excuses like:

Black man: "Girl, you know my tooth is getting ready to come out."

The reason why we're doing it is because we're tired of losing our women to the Latino man. In my book, they're number one. Just give them a bottle of "Adobo" and they'll eat anybody's pussy. This is how things break down ethnically:

1. Puerto Rican men can eat pussy better than any man in America.
2. Black men have the biggest dicks in America.
3. White men have...........full insurance on their cars.

Sweet Revenge

Getting dumped sucks but you never know when sweet revenge will show up. I was on a New York City subway and I saw my ex-girlfriend at the end of the car. That's when sweet revenge revealed its pretty head.

Ex-Girlfriend: "Excuse me, Ladies and Gentlemen. I don't rob or steal. Just trying to get some change so I can get a little sumtin' sumtin' to eat. By the way, for five dollars I'll show you my titties."

White Power!!!

The death of John F. Kennedy, Jr. was a tragic event. It had white people very upset. Personally, I thought it was a tragedy too. But I was proud to see a great show of American power. The rescue effort took five days. They searched high and low, day and night. They had the Coast Guard and the Air Force at work. Even the President got involved. He said, "Stay out there until you find him." When they finally found him, it was indeed a show of American Power.... American white power that is. Because y'all know if it had been Al Sharpton, there would have only been one brother out there searching in a rowboat.

Brother In A Rowboat: "Can I go home now?...I found some curl activator and a red sweat suit."

Taco Fell

What's going on with TACO BELL? The nerve of them, giving a Chihuahua the voice of a Mexican in order to sell tacos. Isn't there a Mexican "Al Sharpton" out there? This is a disgrace to the Mexican people. I'm just glad that Al Sharpton is so vocal because without him these advertisers would probably replace "The Colonel" with a big black monkey. The name "Kentucky Fried Chicken" would be out the door. I can see them in the boardroom battling over the new name:

Bob: "How about we change the name to Magilla Gorilla Fried Chicken?"

Ted: "That's pretty good Bob, but how about this one, Curious George Fried Chicken?"

Bob: "That's good, that's good… But listen to this one…Patrick Ewing Fried Chicken."

Ted: "That's it, that's it, Bob. Wonderful work."

Mr. Bill

The government spent 40 million dollars of our tax money to prove that Monica Lewinsky sucked Bill Clinton's dick. 40 MILLION DOLLARS!!!! The way I see it, I should be able to write off some of that shit on my taxes…Call it a "Monica dickduction." But for those of you who hate Bill Clinton, you have to admit that Monica is also a little crazy. She saved the dress that Mr. Bill ejaculated on. This is not something that a sane woman would do. Maybe she'll save her prom dress or her wedding dress. She would never think to save the dress that some dude jerked off on. What would she brag to her girlfriends about? "Ooooh girl, feel the sleeve, feel how hard the material gets. Girl, he loves me."

Mrs. Bill

Who would you rather get head from…Monica or Hillary? Personally, I'd rather it be Monica. Hillary has those two big buckteeth. It would be like getting the Strawberry Quik rabbit to suck your dick. No thanks. There are two types of women that I don't let suck my dick, bucked tooth women and women with chipped teeth. The unfortunate thing for me is that these are the only women that want to give me head.

Her: "Baby, do you want me to suck it?"
Me: "Noooo thank you…I"ll suck it myself."

Women, fix the chipped ones. You wouldn't like it if I whipped out a chipped dick.

Big Girl

Have you ever wondered why skinny men are drawn to big women? Think about how many times you've seen a woman that weighs 200 pounds holding hands with a man that weighs no more than 125 pounds. I've dated a big woman. Her name was Kathy. She weighed 211 pounds. Everything was going just fine until she decided that we should have sex.

Me: "Kathy, I don't think I'm ready for this?"

Kathy: "Oh, Skinny, you just lay back and let Big Kathy take care of everything."

Me: "No, Kathy, I've changed my mind. Please let me…OHH GOD-DAMN. PLEASE STOP. YOU ARE HURTING ME. YOU'RE TOO HEAVY. MY BALLS ARE IN MY ASS. OH LORD, JESUS, PLEASE HELP ME! YOU'RE TOO BIG. GET OFF."

Two days later.

Kathy: "Skinny, you okay? You think you're ready to get up? You've been in bed for two days."

Me: "I just feel so sore, my legs are so weak. Please…help me find my balls will ya?"

Kathy: "Skinny, you are just so funny. Just lay back and relax. Let me take care of you."

Me: "NO KATHY, NO! NO MORE! PLEASE LORD, JESUS HELP ME……!"

The Civil Rights Movement

I was looking at a documentary on the civil rights movement and I came to the conclusion that Black people back then were a lot stronger than Black people today, myself included. If I was sitting in a restaurant and somebody threw a rock through the window and started yelling, "NIGGER, you can't eat here." I would have probably yelled back, "Okay, okay, I'm leaving. I can't eat anyway since you done bust my teeth out with that rock."

Thong

When the thong came out, I thought it was the sexiest piece of lingerie that a woman could wear. I made sure that my girl had an ample supply of them. Then I did something that I shouldn't have done. I "analyzed" the thong. I came to the conclusion that it's really not quite, well…sanitary. Anything that rests in the crack of your behind shouldn't be used again, EVER! You can't shout that out.

The Israelites

If you're white, don't mess around with the Israelites. Black people don't mess with them, so that should tell you something. I was walking down 42nd Street one afternoon minding my own business when one of the Israelites yelled into the mic:

Israelite: "My Brother…Yeah, you, with the white man's attire on. Come on over here and let me speak to you."

I felt compelled to stop because well……he was one big black motherfucker.

Israelite: "Now brother, step up here on the podium and tell me where are you running off to?"

Me: "Ahh, work."

Israelite: "You work for the white man, don't you? That's the man that enslaved our people. But you feel you need to work for him instead of joining the Israelites and being free. You want to abide by the white man's rules and regulations instead of being the Black American King that you are. You're a Black American King, my brother. You just have to believe that you are. And it's when you believe that you'll start reaping the benefits of a true Black American King. No longer will you have to pay the white man's taxes, you're a king. Leave that shit for the white man. No longer will you have to pay all of that child support, brother. Kings don't pay child support. Those are the white man's rules. No longer will you have to deal with all of those crying babies. You get to plant your seeds wherever you please without all of that interference and hassle. So you see my brother a Black American King is the absolute ruler of his destiny without any of the white man's rules and regulations. You stand here brother with your Brooks Brothers suit on, turning your back to your true attire. Brother under my robe...I am free. Free I tell you! Free of the white man's T-shirt. Free of the white man's drawers. Free of the white man's deodorant. Free brother, free. Join the Israelites and be the King that you are. Now, do you have any questions?"

Me: "Aah yeah, are you really butt naked under that robe? Because it really smells like ass up on this podium."

Rhythm & Blues

What's happening to our Rhythm & Blues singers of today? I went to see the group 702 and K-Ci and Jo-Jo in concert and all I kept hearing them say was *"Come And Help Me Sing It"* or *"If You Know The Song Sing Along."* If I wanted to hear Bubba and Tamika sing, I wouldn't have spent $100.00 for the tickets. I paid to hear yo' ass sing not these motherfuckers sitting next to me.

Man's Best Friend

White people treat their dogs as though they are actual members of the family. They have Health Insurance, 401K and IRA plans set up for their dogs. If the dog happens to get lost, white people go through great lengths to get their dog back. One time I saw a picture of a dog on the back of a milk carton. That is why dogs are a "White Man's Best Friend." I wonder if this statement would have the same meaning if a white family were to hand over their dog to a black family. What do you think?

White Master: "Now Max, we're going away on vacation and we can't take you along this time. My good friend, Wayne Jackson, you remember him, he'll take good care of you. He's the janitor at my firm, boy. He took care of you the last time we went away. I tell you Max that Wayne Jackson, he's the greatest. He can clean the hell out of a garbage can. So cheer up boy and we'll see you in a week."

Max: "No, no! I don't want to stay with Wayne Jackson! Doesn't he live in the South Bronx? Please, let me stay here. Have the neighbors check on me; I'll be fine! Don't leave me with him! He feeds me collard greens and some sort of sweet potato yams that look like my own shit. That's not part of my daily regimen. Last time my intestines were all fucked up. I started farting through my mouth and barking through my ass. Please take me with you. Please Master, please? Wayne doesn't like you and he takes it out on me! He hates the white man. He says that all they do is make him clean out their smelly garbage cans! He watches Malcolm X tapes all day on Saturday and then shoots paper clips at me. Remember that cut above my eye? I didn't scratch myself. That nigger shot me."

White Master: "Boy Max, I've never seen you so excited. You're barking up a storm. Listen boy, being that you're so happy maybe we'll stay two weeks instead of just one."

Max: "Oh my god, this is going to be a "ruff ruff" two weeks."

Relationships

I've given up trying to figure out what women want in a man. With the ever changing trends out there, it's so hard to keep up. Three years ago, I dated a girl that insisted that I go back to school and get my degree. So I did, then the relationship ended. I then met a girl that said she didn't like body hair on her men, so I cut all of my hair, yes, including my ass and pubic hairs. That relationship ended. I am currently dating a girl that claims that she likes her men to be "thugged out." So what did I do? First I beat the shit out of her then I robbed her.

So I guess you're wondering where do I stand now with regards to what women want?

IN JAIL! I got two-five years for the robbery and assault. The hair on my ass, dick and head haven't grown back and I have a college degree that I can't use. Damn!

Latin Lover

Latino men have a reputation for being romantic. They stay with their women through thick and thin. Latino men will shoot the titties off of a woman before letting her run off with someone else. I always wondered how they could love someone so much. Then I dated a Puerto Rican woman and found out. While you're making love to Latino women, they like to put their fingers up your ass. While I was making love to this woman, she stuck her finger up my ass so far that I felt like asking her if she felt any abnormalities in my colon. I stayed in bed all day with the covers over my head. All I kept thinking about is what if someone finds out about this. And just like that I got my answer about why Puerto Rican men go crazy when their women leave them. Their way of thinking is,

Latin Lover: "You're not going to put your finger in my ass, then leave me and start telling people that I enjoyed your finger up my ass. Ohh hell no! I'll cut off all of your toes before I let you do something like that. The way I see it you might as well take off your clothes, get back in bed and put your finger back up my ass because I'm never gonna let you leave me. It's you and me for life, mami."

Time Out

Where did the disciplinary method of using "Time Out" come from? Probably from some old bald-headed psychiatrist without any children. My mother used the "Time Out" approach. But her way of using it was totally different from the way parents use it today.

Mom: "David, I think you need to take a time out. Now go and get Daddy's belt so I can whip yo'ass."

I think all parents should do away with the "Time Out" approach and instead reinstate the "Good Ole Ass-Whipping" approach. I don't want my children to spend any time thinking about anything after I disciplined them. I say give them a spanking and send them back to Toy Land.

Good Ole Ass-Whipping Approach

Mother: "Billy, didn't I tell you to stop hitting your sister?"
POW!

Billy: "I'll stop, Mommy. I promise not to do it again."

Mother: "Okay, don't let me have to hit you again. It hurts me more than it hurts you."

Billy: "Okay, Mom, I love you."

Time-Out Approach

Mother: "Now Billy, I'm going to have to give you a "Time Out." Now come hear and sit down and think about what you've done."

Billy: *"Yeah, that's just what I need. Some time to think about how I'm going to burn this fucking house down. I can't stand it when you interrupt me with this "Time Out" bullshit. Just give me a spanking and let me be on my fucking way. This "Time Out" stuff is cutting into my Pokemon time. As soon as this "Time Out" shit is up, I'm gonna cut all of my sister's hair off and then search the Internet for some explosives."*

Chico

Growing up I was never a big fan of the DeBarge family. Their sound never grabbed me. Then Chico got arrested and did five years in the penitentiary. After he was released from jail, he released one of the best albums of the year. The sound was totally different. It was hardcore, tough with a dash of sensitivity to it. Naturally when his next album dropped I ran out to get it. To my surprise, when I opened the CD cover, there was a picture of Chico in a feather suit laid out like Marilyn Monroe. My first thought was:

What direction are they trying to go with here? Hardcore Gangster Fag? What's up with Motown? If they keep coming up with stupid ideas like this, they'll have to change the name to "HO-MO-TOWN."

If I were Chico, I'd fire the fag that picked that shit out. The way I see it there's only one man on earth that can get away with wearing feathers and that's Prince and only God knows what the hell he is.

Church

I was watching 20/20 the other night and they had a feature story about this Catholic priest named Father Benz. He admitted to police officials on his deathbed that he stole at least $1,000 per week from the collection plate. When the police went to his home, they found gold watches, rings, keys to expensive cars and bundles of empty collection envelopes. When they finished clearing things up, Father Benz had taken the Catholic Church for over $1 million dollars. The funny thing about this situation is that the white people in the congregation did not seem too upset. They even took care of the priest's funeral arrangements and buried his white ass at the same church that he robbed.

Now this shit would have never have happened in a Black Church. HELL NO! First of all, any minister that is appointed to the Black Church using the name Reverend Benz, Pastor Cadillac or Bishop Lincoln would be thrown out before he could even take the first collection. Black churches are broke as shit. Black parishioners don't have money like white parishioners. White parishioners follow the rules. They give the church 10% of their gross pay as tithes. Black parishioners have excuses like:

Black Parishioner: "Fuck that, I'm behind in my rent. God is gonna just have to understand. All I can afford right now is a nickel."

Black Minster: "I told you that the roof was gonna come down on us. Look over there at Sister Washington. She's dead. Now will ya give me the money?"

I figured out why white people give so much to the church. They're trying to buy God's love. They think that money will help God forget whatever bad deeds they have done.

White Parishioner: "God, I'm sorry for cheating on my wife. Please forgive me. But on a lighter note, we're getting bonuses at the office, that means that I'll definitely be able to give you that 10% this year. I might even be able to throw in a little extra assuming that you can forget about that blow job my secretary gave me last week.... Amen."

Gay Test

There is a test that men can take that will tell them if they are gay. To take this test, please hand this book over to a friend and have your friend read the following to you:

GAY TEST

Close your eyes and imagine yourself on a beach. You're lying on the sand on your belly with a thong on. A big muscular guy comes over to you and asks you if you would like for him to put some suntan lotion on your back and buttocks…

If your eyes are still closed at this point, the test is over. You're a fag!

The WNBA

The WNBA must stand for "Women With No Beauty At All." The women in the WNBA have to be the ugliest women on the face of the planet. They need to change the name to W-UGLY-A. Aren't there any Halle Berry's out there playing basketball? Damn! I feel like I'm watching men with titties. I was watching a game and I thought that I saw my uncle on the lay-up line. Then my boy said, "No man, that's Cheryl Swoops." And Cynthia Cooper with those big black eyes may be the MVP but in my book she's the MVR—MOST VALUABLE RACCOON. However, they do have one pretty one, Lisa Leslie. Isn't it funny how she is the only one that does commercials? In fact, she does them for every WNBA team.

Conspiracy Theory

Whenever there is an unfortunate situation in the black community and white people are involved, you can bet that not too far behind there will be a Black leader yelling out the words, "This is a **Conspiracy** against the Black man!" And if you have any doubts or questions about this so-called "Conspiracy," you can be sure that the Leader will have the time to break it down for you. Remember when the Space Shuttle exploded in mid-air for all of America to see? Well, I heard one so called "Black leader" preaching on the streets about the incident. His analogy was a lot different from what the newspapers had to say.

Black Leader: "Say my brother, did you hear about the explosion?"

Me: "Yes, I heard about it. It's really sad."

Black Leader: "No my brother it's not sad. It's a Conspiracy to keep the Black man down. And when I say down, I mean down. They've been sending them space ships up for years and nothing like this has ever happened. As soon as they send a nigga up there the shit blows up. I'm telling you man Whitey don't want niggas going to the moon."

Me: "Man, that's got to be the dumbest shit I've ever heard."

Black Leader: "My brother, it's obvious that your eyes are closed. You can't see the truth. It's like my great grandfather would say, "Those who walk with their eyes shut will one day end up with Jackass Balls.""

Me: "Jackass Balls? Man, what the hell are you talking about?"

Black Leader: "Well, to tell you the truth, I don't know. I told you this was something that my great grandfather would say. But let me break this thing down for you. Do you know what NASA stands for?"

Me: "Yes, National Aeronautics and Space Administration."

Black Leader: "Wrong brother, wrong! This is what NASA stands for,

The "N" stands for	NO
The "A" stands for	AFRICAN AMERICANS
The "S" stands for	SEEN
The "A" stands for	AFTER

What does this all mean? It means no African Americans will be seen after we leave! Them whiteys is planning on fixing the moon up real nice. They already have cable and shit up there. They are planning to leave earth one day and live on the moon, man. Brothers like you and I will be left here on this hell hole we call Earth. And the reason why they picked the moon is because it's as white as can be. There might be darkness around the moon, but there's no color within it. It's gonna be one big white planet with no niggas. I'm telling you brother, this is a conspiracy to keep the Black man down...on earth."

Self-Help

There are so many self-help books out there. One that seems to be leading the pack is the book called "One Day My Soul Just Opened" by Iyanla Vazant. I purchased her book and found that it didn't quite answer the questions I had about my relationship with my girlfriend. It was missing vital answers to questions like:

"How can I get my girlfriend to let me masturbate in the living room once in awhile?"

"How do I get my girlfriend to shut her fucking mouth without hitting her?"

"How can I get my girlfriend to ask one of her fine girlfriends to join us in some wild sex?"

See, these are the things that men want to learn about, not any of that "How to keep your relationships strong" crap. We can learn that from our mothers.

Don't Blame Hillary

Everyone blames Hillary Clinton for the President's infidelity. They say that she wasn't "taking care of business" in the bedroom. What people fail to realize is that Bill was asking her to do some unconstitutional shit.

Bill: "Honey, can I stick a slice of pizza up your pussy?"

Hillary: "No!"

Bill: "Okay, then how about letting me put this Cuban Cigar up your ass? It's a good one. I got it from Fidel Castro."

Family Life

My son goes to a racially mixed Junior High School. Last semester he brought one of his white friends over to hang out and play video games. For the first time in my life, I screened a white kid.

Me: "Hello, Billy. I just have a few questions that I need to ask you before you guys get started with your game, okay?"

Billy: "Ahh sure, Mr. Asbery."

Me: "Have you ever ordered large quantities of Ether, Gunpowder, or Flammable liquids of any kind over the Internet?"

Billy: "No, Mr. Asbery."

Me: "Has your father ever molested you? And if so, would you kill him and your mother if you could get away with it? You know sort of like what the Menendez brothers did?"

Billy: "No, Mr. Asbery. That's ridiculous."

Me: "Okay Billy, this is the last question. On the 4th of July, do you play with sparklers or M80's? Now be honest Billy."

Billy: "Well Mr. Asbery, one year my friends and I set off one of those M80's but it was just one…"

Me: "Get the fuck out of my house! You're not going to blow my fucking house up. Little David, you bring some niggas home to play with. Fuck these white boys. They're all crazy!"

Don't Get Them Mad

I'm not looking to piss off too many white people these days. Their anger is worse than black folks. If you piss off a black person, you can be sure that he's either gonna whip your ass or curse your mother out then whip your ass. White people, on the other hand, go overboard! They'll blow up your next door neighbor's house and then write you a letter telling you that your house is next. But the thing that really bothers me is how patient white people can be when they're mad at you. They can hold off their anger for long periods of time. They will threaten you today and blow your house up four months later. One day you'll come home from a hard day's work not even thinking about that white man that you cursed out at the toll booth five months ago. You'll turn on the television, flip the channel to BET and VA BOOM! All of your shit is blown the fuck up.

Gangsta Rappers

I love Gangsta Rappers. Every single thing that they do is expressed in a hardcore format. I went to a benefit where a Rapper was being honored. His acceptance speech was off the hook.

Rapper: "Yo, Yo, I'd like to thank all you motherfuckers for making this shit possible. I'd also like to thank my main man, Shoot em Up. He wrote the first track on my platinum selling album, "Blow Up the Fucking White House But Don't Forget to Fuck Chelsea." Yeah, yeah, and last but not least, I'd like to thank The Creator, My Lord and Savior Jesus Christ. He's the motherfucker that made it possible for me to be here. I'm getting mo' pussy and got mo' money than all you motherfuckers out here and I gots Him to thank for dat shit. I'm here to testify that The Creator will answer all, not some, but all of yo' motherfucking prayers. Ya see, I prayed for all of the Haters to be dead and with his guidance and a little help from my man, Shoot-Em Up, all them niggas is dead. One more thing yo, I got a new album coming out. I'm trying to do something a little different, trying to be more mature with this one here. Because you know, I'm fully aware that the inner city kids be listening to my music and well...I gots kids too. I don't take care of them but I gots them. Anyway, my new album is

called, "I'LL FUCK YO' MAMA IN THE ASS." It'll be released off of
RECTUM RECORDS. Yeah, yeah."

TAE-BO (Billy Banks)

When the TAE-BO tapes by Billy Banks first came out, my girlfriend wanted them so bad that she took down the 1-800 number and demanded that I order them for her. When I got on the phone with one of the TAE-BO representatives, I asked them for the price including shipping. For 4 tapes the total came to about $65.00. I instantly hung up the telephone and told my girl that they were all sold out and that I would try again. My thinking was, *Fuck Billy Banks. $65.00 is too much for the working guy to pay for some fucking tapes.* About a week later I bumped into this Hispanic brother that was standing on the corner of 125th Street in Harlem. He had the entire TAE-BO collection for the low price of $20.00. I asked the brother, "Why are your prices so low?" His answer, "Fuck Billy Banks. $65.00 is too much for the working guy to pay for some fucking tapes." I purchased the tapes and surprised my girlfriend after dinner and man, did we have a beautiful evening. The next morning my girlfriend woke up at 6:00 a.m. eager to work out. She put on her workout gear and asked me if I wanted to do TAE-BO with her. I thought, *Why the fuck would I want to wake up and see some ugly motherfucker jumping around? If you want to wake me up for something, wake me up to suck my dick.*

Well, anyway, I went back to sleep. About 30 seconds later my girl-friend was pulling the covers off of me yelling and screaming.

Girlfriend: "What the fuck is this BULLSHIT?"
Me: "What, what?"
Girlfriend: "THIS BULLSHIT ON THE TAPE YOU BOUGHT ME!"

When I got up to look at the tape, instead of seeing Billy Banks working out it was the Hispanic brother that sold me the tape. He had three fat women and a midget doing jumping jacks. They were working out to Ricky Martin's song, *Livin' La Vida Loca.* There really wasn't too much to say to my girlfriend at that point. I just picked up the telephone, dialed the 1-800 number, and ordered the TAE-BO tapes for $65.00. Then I dialed another 1-800 number and ordered her a bracelet for $500.00.

BET Is Unrealistic

The commercials on BET are so unrealistic. They're just white commercials with black actors reciting the lines. They need to change the format and BE REAL. Check out this ad for washing detergent.

Unrealistic Black Commercial on BET

Black Mother: "Billy, you've soiled your pants. Now take them off so that I can wash them and get that awful stain out."

Realistic Black Commercial on BET

Black Mother: "Leroy, you done shit on yourself again. Didn't I tell you to take your motherfucking pants off before you shit? Boy, you just as crazy as your Uncle Lewis. Damn, ya done got yourself all fucked up. Well don't even think of putting them in the hamper cause I ain't washing shit until Saturday."

Mother Love

I can't stomach Mother Love. She is such an instigator. She exposes and exploits people for ratings. Unlike the other talk shows, she tries to convince the viewers that she's pouring out *Motherly Love.*

Mother Love: "Brenda, you just found out that your husband had oral sex with your sister the night before your wedding. Do you think you'll be able to forgive and forget?"

Brenda: "Well, Mother Love, that was a long time ago. I'm now divorced from him and my sister has changed her ways. She's my best friend."

Mother Love: "So you mean to tell me that yo' sister, sucked yo man's dick the day before you got married and you don't have a problem with it? You is one stupid bitch. There's no way that I could forgive her for something like that."

Brenda: "Well…"

Mother Love: "So when you were kissing your man on your wedding day, in actuality, you were kissing yo' sister's…We can't say pussy on the air y'all…uhh vagina. Dat's some nasty stuff, honey."

Brenda: "You know something Mother Love, you're right. Why should I forgive that bitch? She's always trying to take my stuff. I'm gonna kick her ass after the show."

Mother Love: "Brenda, I thank you for sharing your story with us and always remember…Never underestimate the power of an ass whipping when someone does you wrong!"

Shave It!

I ate dinner with a business associate of mine last week and while we were eating I noticed his nose and ear hairs were extremely long. They were so long that he could have braided them all together. It made me wonder about my hairs so when I got home that night I looked at all of my body hairs. When I finally got to my behind, it scared the shit out of me. It looked like I had a horsetail attached to my ass!

School Bus Driver

This is a job that you can keep. When kids ride on those yellow school buses, they lose their minds. I think they should release the "Scared Straight" guys from jail and let them drive our kids to school.

Scared Straight Guy: "Billy, what the fuck are you doing back there? If you get out of your seat one more fucking time, you're gonna be my bitch for the rest of the ride. Hey, hey, Jamarl bring yo' punk ass to the front of the bus and give me all of your motherfucking Pokémon cards. Hey Brenda, did you finish your English homework? 'Cause if you didn't, you're gonna have to hold my dick again. Hey, hey, Michael, why every time I talk to you, ya pee on yourself? You got a fucking problem or something? I'm telling you right now, ain't none of y'all getting out of this cell…I mean off this bus until this motherfucker is clean."

After being with the Scared Straight guy, your kid would be glad to be in school. Their grades would probably go through the ceiling.

Watch What You Wear

I was on my way to a club when this crackhead approached me. He pulled me to the side and said,

Crackhead: "Hey man, for $5.00 I'll lick your ass."

Me: "Well, damn…, what would you do for $10.00?"

At first, I got mad that he approached me but then I started judging myself. What did I have on to make this crackhead think that I wanted my ass licked?

The Black Man

The black woman is the most beautiful creature on this earth. Their beauty stems from within and graces us all like the heat from the sun on a brisk cold day. The black woman's inner spirit has proven to be so strong that it can lift and enlighten the black man to great lengths. A black man that is down in the depths of hell only need to ask the black woman and she will share her innermost strengths and uplift the black man, giving him power that he needs and the confidence to seek out and conquer his dreams....

A lovely home, a fancy car and an ugly white woman.

Oral Sex

At one time in my life I loved giving Oral Sex. I thought that it was the most beautiful thing that a man could do to a woman. To see your woman laying on her back unable to argue or run her mouth is in my opinion worth the effort. Then one day an incident occurred that would forever change my views on Oral Sex. After a romantic dinner with my girlfriend, we went into the bedroom for…Well, I don't have to spell it out. Let's just say that I had my mouth full. While I was "down" on her, she was in ecstasy.

Her: "Ohhh, David. Ohhh."

Me: "Lick, lick, slurp, slurp, lick."

Her: "Oh, God. It's so good."

Me: "Lick, lick, kiss, slurp."

Her: "Ohh, my God, it's coming. I'm gonna let it go."

Me: "Let it go baby; enjoy yourself."

Her: "Okay baby, here it comes."

My girlfriend farted so long and so loud; I'm still having problems hearing out of my left ear. I looked up at her and said, "What the hell was that?" What's your problem? When she said that she was "gonna let it go," I didn't know that she was talking about a fart. This was only the beginning of my problems. It's hard enough trying to get the smell of vagina out of your mustache. Try getting the smell of vagina and a fart out and you'll understand my dilemma. My head stunk for about a week. That Monday morning, I walked into my office and my boss told me to take my ass back home. He said that I smelled like I had my head inside of a baboon's ass.

The Crying Game

My ex-wife was a crier. She would cry about everything. When I first met her, I thought she was just sensitive. I would later find out that she was crazy. One time I called her at home from work to tell her that I was going out. Here is an example of what I had to deal with:

Me: "Honey, I'm meeting up with Seymour after work today."

Her: "OOH NO! I KNOW YOU'RE NOT COMING BACK. YOU'RE GONNA LEAVE ME. PLEASE DON'T GOOOOOOOOOO. BOO HOO, BOO, HOO, OH JESUS! PLEASE, AWWWWWW LAWD. I KNOW YOU'RE NOT COMING BACK!"

Me: "Okay, okay. I won't go. I'll come straight home."

The bad thing about being in a relationship like that is that you end up mentally damaged. You end up carrying bad luggage into your next relationship. My next relationship ended in less than a week.

Me: "Hey, baby… What's wrong, why are you crying?"

My New Girl: "I just got a call…My Dad… He died."

Me: "DAMN, what the fuck are you crying for? Everybody got to die sometime. You knew the Nigga was gonna die anyway. Shit, he's been in and out of the hospital for months. Damn, move on already!"

Six Ways to Piss the NAACP Off

1. Use the word "I" in front of the word "be" such as: "I be going to the rally or I be getting along with them fine."
2. Start a letter campaign urging the networks to give "Homeboys In Outer Space" another chance.
3. Ask them how much money did Hazel Dukes steal from them.
4. Insist that Denny's be the official sponsor for all NAACP up and coming events.
5. Eat a big ole watermelon at any NAACP event.
6. Tell them that they are wrong about David Duke and that you think that he's just trying to help us as a people.

Mr. Rudy Giuliani

After almost two terms in office, New York City Mayor, Rudolph Giuliani has decided to crack down on taxicab drivers that refuse to pick up black people. This move was personal. He didn't do it to be politically correct in any way. This is what really happened:

Mayor: "Where is that nigger Cleophus? That's why I don't have any niggers on my staff now. They keep that aah, aah, what do they call it? Oh yeah, "Colored Peoples Time." I sent that boy across town an hour ago to pick me up some Krispy Kreme donuts and coffee. I even gave him cab fare."

Cleophus comes in with the Krispy Kreme bag. He's all out of breath.

Mayor: "Cleophus, where the hell have you been boy?"

Cleophus: "I's sorry, Mr. Rudy Giuliani, Sir. I's tried my best to gets yo' coffee back here on time. It just that I's couldn't catch a cab on account that I's Black, Mr. Rudy Giuliani, Sir. I's really sorry 'bout this. I's go and microwave yo' coffee nice and quick for ya, Mr. Rudy Giuliani, Sir."

Mayor: "Cleophus, get that microwave shit out of my face. What's this city coming to when a nigger can't catch a cab to get me my coffee. Damn. Did you tell the cab driver that you was going on an errand for the Mayor of New York City?"

Cleophus: "Yes, Mr. Giuliani, Sir, I's sure did."

Mayor: "Well, what did he say?"

Cleophus: "Well, he said the I's a liar because the Mayor of this great here city don't have no nigger on his staff. Then he got out of his cab and kicked me in my britches."

Kirk Franklin's Going to Hell

I don't want to be anywhere near Kirk Franklin when they hand out the tickets at the Pearly Gates because he's going to HELL! God doesn't like what his version of gospel music is doing to people. I was at a nightclub and the song *STOMP* came on and the women went wild. One women pulled me out on the dance floor and started rubbing her breasts and buttocks up against me, dancing all close. I stopped dancing and pulled her to the side.

Me: "Hey, Girl, you can't be dancing like this. This song is praising our Lord Savior, Jesus Christ."
Girl: "Nigga, please."

She just walked off making her own lyrics to the song:

"Rub my bootie now…STOMP"
"Rub my titties now…STOMP."

Black History Month

I'm totally for teaching black youth about Black History. However, I feel that it should be taught throughout the year instead of setting aside one month. Ramming all of this information into our kids can cause more harm than good.

Me: "Hey, David Jr. Come here."

My son: "What's up, dad?"

Me: "How much is 5x5?"

My Son: "Ahh, 5x5?"

Me: "Yeah, how much is 5x5?"

My Son: "Ahhhhh, I know. 5x5= Martin Luther King, Jr. No, no, wait. 5x5=Harriet Tubman? Marcus Garvey? No, it's Rosa Parks. Yeah, that's it. 5x5 = Rosa Parks. Come on dad, hit me with another one."

Me: "Shit!"

Learn to Wash

I'm a firm believer that men don't really know how to wash. Because females are the only ones that I can get to read my material, I get to hear about the problems that they have with their men. It seems like they all complain about the same thing. **Hygiene.** I hear things like:

"I ain't sucking that shit no more. His balls smell like sardines."

or

"What's wrong with him? Can't he properly clean his ass? He has logs of shit in his drawers. He's so nasty."

After hearing this, I went home that night and stepped in the shower with my girl.

My Girl: "Hi baby, you don't usually take a shower with me. This is nice."

Me: "Yeah, this is nice baby. Listen, do you mind washing me tonight? I'm a little tired."

My girl picked up the scrub brush and a bottle of Tilex and started scrubbing my ass and balls so hard you would have thought she was trying to get some spray paint off of a New York City subway. You think she was trying to tell me something?...NAW.

"HONEY WHAT'S WRONG? YOU LOOK LIKE YOU'RE GONNA PASS OUT!!"

Pokémon

My children are among the gazillion kids that are Pokémon fiends. The cards cost up to $10.00 per pack. And the scary thing about this is that my kids can never get enough of them. It's like they're on crack. You should see my kids when they come across another kid that has Pokémon cards. They turned into Los Vegas gamblers.

My Son: "I'll trade you my Pokémon red cards for your Pikachu card. But you have to give me two Ponyta cards first. If you give me the Ponyta card, I'll give you a Pidgeotto card next week."

One time my youngest son pulled out a cigarette and started smoking while trading. He explained to me that it was just to set the mood. I guess I shouldn't be too upset at Pokémon because there's another "P" word that can get them in more trouble. Pussy. If they start trading that back and forth, I could end up with two pimps by the time they graduate.

74

The Judicial System

The American judicial system has to be the worst system in the world. The time and the money that is wasted in court is amazing. You have judges postponing cases and attorneys asking for continuances. By the time the case comes to court, all of the facts are forgotten. That's why I think that football officials should take over and run the judicial system. Imagine the little men in black and white running into the courtroom ready to referee a case:

John Madden: "Okay, Ladies and Gentlemen, our first case has to do with a black man beating the hell out of a white man. Here comes the officials."

Football Officials: "OKAY....WE HAVE A PENALTY RULING. CASE NUMBER 5783, BLACK MAN ROUGHING THE MASTER...THAT'LL BE A FIVE YEAR PENALTY. THAT'S ONE DOWN."

John Madden: "Wow, Ladies and Gentlemen, the officials are on the ball today. We already got the first one down. Let's move on to our next case. In this case, the plaintiff has made allegations that she was raped.

Football Officials: "OKAY...WE HAVE A PENALTY RULING. CASE NUMBER 5087, WHITE MAN. WE HAVE HOLDING. HOLDING

THE WOMAN DOWN. THAT'LL BE A TEN YEAR PENALTY. THAT'S THE SECOND ONE DOWN."

John Madden: "Holy cow, he got ten years. The fans are really satisfied with that one…Let's see an instant replay of his face after the ruling. Boy, he looks mad. Okay, folks, that's a rap for today. But before we go, we have some highlights from the other courtrooms around the city. Let's get right into the action."

Football Officials: "Okay, we have a false start…it's an illegal search and seizure and a personal foul charge to the white officer against the black man. That will be a $50,000 penalty against the officer and another $50,000 against the City."

John Madden: "Wow, a black man can get rich while driving his car. Boy, let's check out Cleophus' face after the officials made their decision. Boy, is he ever happy. The officer was really out of bounds on that play. Well, that's it folks. The calendar is cleared. This is John Madden signing off and please remember folks, when asked what the NFL stands for, yell out:

N	=	NO
F	=	FELONS
L	=	LOOSE
N	=	NO
F	=	FELONS
L	=	LOOSE

Court's adjourned.

Five Steps to Total Happiness

Have you ever made love to your woman until she cried? I have and I can tell you that it's the most beautiful thing in the world. For those of you who have never experienced this, here is a step-by-step guide to achieving this delightful sensuous feeling.

Step One: Greet your woman at the door with a soft gentle kiss when she comes home from work.

Step Two: Have dinner cooked for her. Maybe some seafood and white wine. Seafood will help stimulate your woman and the wine will relax her, putting her in a sensuous mood.

Step Three: After dinner, put on a Luther Vandross CD. Make sure you program your CD player so that only the slow love songs play.

Step Four: Dim the lights and kiss her gently, teasing her with your tongue. Just as she is about to pull you closer, pull away and whisper, "Baby, you are love and I need love right now."

Step Five: Make passionate love to your woman and just as she is about to climax open your eyes and watch as salty tears slowly roll down the sides of her face.

Man, I'm telling you this has to be the most beautiful thing in the world.

P.S. If none of this shit works, turn her over and fuck her in the ass dry. Either way you'll end up with some tears.

The Split

I'm glad that my wife and I had the sense to split up. If we didn't make this decision, someone would have gotten hurt. I mean it got so bad that I started checking my meals. I would pick at my rice, grain by grain, and squeeze it just to make sure that there wasn't any glass in it. I remember one time my wife and I were at the dinner table waiting for our kids to join us. After the food was served, I switched my son's plate with mine, right in front of her face. She just sat there and shook her head. At that point, I started to feel a little sorry for my actions. Our kids came to the table and we all blessed the food. As I reached over to apologize to my wife, my son simultaneously picked up his fork. That's when my wife yelled out:

"JAMARL, DON'T EAT THAT FOOD! THERE'S POISON IN IT!!!"

After this outburst, my wife looked over at me and smiled like she was posing for a picture or something.

Movie Deal

I'm in the process of writing a movie about slavery. In one of the scenes, there's a slave that gets caught trying to run away. The Slave Master cuts off his legs. The slave tries to run away again. The Slave Master cuts off his arms. By the end of the movie, the only thing left on the slave is an EYE. But he's free. I think I'll call it, "EYE IS FREE."

John Glenn

White America loves any type of heartwarming stories that can balloon into a worldwide historical event. When they sent John Glenn into space, my first thought was, *NASA wants this old fart to die in space.* This would be the ultimate send-off and would make John Glenn a name to remember forever. I'd like to hear the conversations that Glenn had with the other astronauts. I'm sure everything wasn't as smooth as NASA wants us to believe. You know how old people can be sometimes especially the ones that have been to the moon and back. You can't tell them anything!

Astronaut: "NASA, we're ready to flip switch number seven."

John Glenn: "I think you should wait before you hit that switch, son."

Astronaut: "But I checked with NASA. They said if we're clear, we can flip the switch."

John Glenn: "But you didn't check with me, son. I have sixty years of experience with these switches. That's the problem with you young whippersnappers. You're so quick with everything. When I was your age, I would always listen to my father. He taught me patience, son. Something you need more of. Drinking all of that Gatorade got your

81

mind all scrambled. You need to start drinking Tang. That's what a real astronaut is supposed to drink. That stuff will make your stool nice and soft."

NASA: "John, we need you to pursue command. Your comrade's inability to flip that switch has set us back."

Asronaut: "See what you did, ya old fart, ya got me in trouble."

I Cheated

After about eight years of hiding the truth from my wife, I broke down and told her that I cheated on her. Now why did I go and do that? I really wasn't ready for my wife's reaction to this news:

Wife: "YOU VIOLATED THE TRUST!"

Me: "NO......I..."

Wife: "DAVID, YOU HURT ME BEYOND REPAIR."

Me: "NO, HONEY, I JUST...."

Wife: "YOU WERE TRYING TO DESTROY ME, WEREN'T YOU? I'VE BEEN PUBLICLY HUMILIATED. IS THAT WHAT YOU WERE TRYING TO DO?"

Me: "NO, NO. I JUST WANTED TO GET MY ASS LICKED, MY DICK SUCKED. THAT'S ALL....HONEST."

Wife: "WELL, WHY DIDN'T YOU COME TO ME?"

Me: "HONEY, YOU KISS THE KIDS. I COULDN'T ASK YOU TO DO THAT. YOU'RE TOO GOOD FOR THAT."

Nina

When it comes to women I have no luck. I used to date this girl named Nina that had these sudden attacks. These seizures. The very first one occurred after our first sexual encounter. I remember being on top of her and hearing her yell out, "YOU'RE THE GREAT-EST." I remember thinking to myself, *Wow, that's a first…Women usually say to me, "IS THAT IT?" or "Damn, I didn't even finish taking my clothes off."* But not Nina. She was satisfied and because of that I was in love. As we layed on our backs, panting from this glorious sexual experience, I looked over at Nina and noticed that she was shaking. I assumed that she was having one of those multiple orgasms that women talk so much about but can't seem to have. It wasn't until all of that spit and slob started popping out of her head that I realized, *SOMETHING IS WRONG!* I remember thinking, *Damn, this multiple orgasm thing can be harmful.* After rushing her to the hospital and telling her doctor my version of what happened to Nina. The Doctor told me in a rather crass manner, "Sir, please don't pat yourself on the back. This had nothing to do with sex. Nina had a seizure, you idiot!"

Ex-wife

My Youngest son, Jamarl, was very upset when my wife and I separated. After being together for all eight years of his life he just couldn't understand why we couldn't resolve our differences. I remember one day he walked over to me and asked,

Jamarl: "Dad...What's an orgasm?"

Me: "What?"

Jamarl: "An orgasm dad, an orgasm."

Me: "Where did you hear that word?"

Jamarl: "I heard it from mom. She was talking to someone on the telephone and she said that you couldn't give her one and that's the reason why she left you.... Dad, I have an idea. I'll save up my allowance and help you buy an orgasm."

He's Still Prince to Me

Prince is doing a hell of a lot of talking these days. There once was a time when you couldn't get a word out of him. Now he won't shut the fuck up! I think that Prince is a lonely man. You can look at him and tell that he is very antsy and the average guy would get tired of hanging with him because, well, he has a girl at home that's the same way. I mean think about it. Have you ever seen Prince hanging out with any male celebrities? Take Chris Rock for example. Chris will interview him but you won't ever hear Chris say that he called Prince up to go out shopping.

Chris: "Hey, Prince, are you almost finished? I have to get back."

Prince: "Yeah, Chris. I just have to make one more stop."

Victotia Secrets Manager: "Hello, Prince. Your order came in today. That's seven purple thongs, four purple panty and bra sets, and one pair of high heel pinked slippers."

Chris: "Hey, Prince, who's the lucky girl?"

Prince: "What do you mean lucky girl? This shit is mine…Awoooh oooh."

New Year's Resolution

My New Year's Resolution was to become the first black person to win the Publishers Clearing House Sweepstakes. For some reason the van never seems to come to my neighborhood. I've realized that if the truck ever showed up in my neighborhood, we'd be the ones *clearing house.* I guess it's best that they don't come. I don't trust those two guys anyway. Dicky Clark and fat ass Ed Mc Muffin.

What the Hell Goes On In There?

What goes on in the public ladies restroom? Whenever I go to a night club, a movie or restaurant with my girl, the line to the ladies restroom is always crowded with about 50 women waiting to get in. I just find it hard to believe that they're all in there attempting to urinate. There must be some big dick dude in there sitting on the toilet seat naked. That would explain why they always go in pairs and come back looking so happy and relieved.

Being Black

If you're black and in the public eye, don't screw up because white people will never let you forget it. Take for example major league baseball player Doc Gooden.

Announcer: "Boy, fans, one more strike and it's a no-hitter for the Doc....And he gets the strike. That's a new major league record. Doc Gooden has struck out every single batter that has come to the plate. I'm sure he's gonna celebrate tonight. Oh yeah, he'll probably get his crack pipe, call Darryl Strawberry and get fucked up!!!"

Jennifer Lopez

I just read that Jennifer Lopez has insured her body for a whopping $1 million. So what does this mean? If someone bumps into her at a club, she can put in a claim. Now that she has this insurance policy, she's out of my fantasy book. No longer will I dream about sleeping with her. There's just too much pressure now. What if we're making love and she doesn't climax? Can she sue me for the insufficient use of her body? What if I fuck her so good that she can't walk the next day? Will her insurance representative have to examine my penis? God forbid her ass gets flat. All of our premiums will probably go up. I just hope that this is not a trend because a lot of women will end up getting their feelings hurt.

Insurance Representative: "I'm sorry, Ms. Jones, but at this time we won't be able to insure you. There are just too many sexual partners in your history. And with all of those stretch marks, your body just isn't worth insuring. However, may I interest you in some Coco Butter?"

Smoke

Phillip Morris is trying to help stop the growing number of teenage kids from smoking. They are running television advertisements asking kids to explain why they refuse to smoke, hoping to discourage other kids from smoking. Since these ads are live, I'm sure they must run into one oddball:

Phillip Morris: "Hey, hey, kid. Yeah, you."

Kid: "Yeah, what's up?"

Phillip Morris: "Do you smoke?"

Kid: "Yes, what's it to you?"

Phillip Morris: "Oh, aah, well, we're trying to get kids to stop smoking by finding out why they started."

Kid: "Well is that all you want to know, why I started smoking?"

Phillip Morris: "Yes."

Kid: "Well, you should have said so. It started back in 1972 when my mother left me at a foster home. At age 4, I was adopted by a Puerto Rican family that spoke no English and ate nothing but cornmeal for breakfast, lunch and dinner. At 15, I ran away and tried to find my father. When I finally found him, he was on crack and asked to borrow $5.00. I never got around to going to school because I've been working so that I can eat."

Phillip Morris: "Damn, you really need cigarettes. Here, take my pack."

Black Leadership

I think that Martin Luther King, Jr. was the strongest out of all the black leaders. I mean if you look at Malcolm X or Huey Newton, these brothers were able to release their hostility. Martin had to suck it up and walk around with it. I mean check out the way these three men viewed things:

MALCOLM'S VIEW

"If the white man throws a rock at your window, you pick up the biggest rock and throw it at that white man's mother's window, and you keep throwing rocks at his mother's window until he leaves you alone."

MARTIN'S VIEW

"If the white man throws a rock at your church window, fix the window and pray. If the white man throws another rock at that same window, fix the window and pray harder brothers and sisters, for they know not what they are doing. If the white man throws a load of dynamite through that same window again, get the hell out. You are in the wrong neighborhood. We'll build another church somewhere else!"

I just don't believe that Martin was able to get up everyday after being thrown in jail or hit in the head with a rock and not be a little angry. I think that Martin had two versions of the *I Have A Dream* speech. The one that was televised for America to see and the one that he made special, an unedited version for blacks only.

"I have a dream that one day, I'll be able to find those white fireman that blasted Brother Jenkins' ass all the way down Montgomery Avenue. I have a dream, that one day, my son will grow up and whip little Tommy's ass for calling him a nigger on stage at his high school play. I have a dream today y'all, that one day I'll be able to walk around in a pair of jeans and throw away this polyester suit. I have a dream this morning ya'll that one day we'll rise as a people and beat whitey's ass! Beat whitey's ass! Please Lord Jesus, let us beat whitey's ass!"

Ten Things That Piss Black People Off

1. **The Tawana Brawley Story.** Black Person: "Man, that bitch is full of shit."

2. **Diana Ross' hair.** Black Person: "Man, her head must weigh about five pounds!"

3. **Potato Salad without Mustard, Relish, Black Pepper, Onions & Paprika.** Black people will label your salad "White People's Potato Salad" if any one of these ingredients are missing.

4. **The fact that every brother that you meet on the street is a producer with an album coming out in June.**

5. **Too much help in a department store.**

   White Store Clerk #1: "Can I help you?"

   Black Customer: "No, I'm just looking."

   White Store Clerk #2: "Can I help you, sir?"

   Black Customer: "No thanks. I'm just looking."

   White Store Clerk #3: "Sir, can I help you?"

Black Customer: "No God damn-it! Can't a nigga just look... Damn!"

White Store Clerk: *Yeah, you can look, but once in a while buy something.*

6. **Not enough help in a department store.**

    Black Customer: "Will someone please help me?"

    White Store Clerk: "Never mind him. He was here last week and asked me if we had a lay-a-way plan."

7. **An interview with singer James Brown.** Black Person: "Just have that nigga sing and sit the fuck down. I can't understand a word he's saying if he ain't singing."

8. **Jennifer Lopez's ass.** Black Women: "They're giving that bitch too much credit. We had big round asses before anyone was thinking of them. Back in 1842, they used to call my grandmother, Big Ass Martha."

9. **Black men that didn't make it to the Million Man March.** Black Man's excuse for not attending the March: "Man, the reason why I wasn't there is because I thought that this would be the perfect day to try and get some extra pussy."

10. **White Diva's.** Black Person: "Yeah, I agree, she can sing but she can't *sang*. Patty Labelle can *sang*."

Ten Things That Piss White People Off

1. **The Tawana Brawley story.** White Man: "Man she put us through the ringer with that whopper. I missed the "Air Supply" concert because I was scared to leave the house.

2. **Fat women in Gospel Choirs that sing lead.** White Person: "Why the hell do they have to sing so loud? I never read anything in the Bible about God being deaf!"

3. **The two letters, "O" and "J."**

4. **Potato Salad with Mustard, Relish, Black Pepper, Onions & Paprika.** White Person: "This shit taste more like Cube Steak than Potato Salad."

5. **When there are no black people in a department store.** White Person: "Shit, I can't steal today…No decoys."

6. **That their kids actually like rap music.** White Dad: "Now Bobby, you want me to pick up the CD entitled "Kill Whitey All Day Long" by The Nat Turner Crew?"

7. **Jennifer Lopez's ass.** White Model: "Shit, all of these years I spent working out trying to keep my ass flat and now having a big ass is in style."

8. **Diana Ross' hair.**

9. **Hailing a cab on a busy street and three cabs crash into each other trying to pick you up.**

10. **Playing golf.......with black people.**

Mr. Gary Coleman

Gary Coleman really has it bad. Not only did he blow millions of dollars, he never thought of using some of the money to get blown. I saw Gary on one of those *Where Are They Now Specials*. He was practically begging for pussy. He said that he's still a virgin and that he's pretty damn tired of it. Well Gary's not the only one that's tired. I'm tired of all of his begging and complaining. He used to be a nice little guy. Now he's an angry frustrated asshole. If he would just shut up for a minute, I'm sure that there's someone out there that would give him some pussy. Once you get pass those little pork sausage fingers, how bad could it be?

Todd Bridges used drugs, shot at people, was in and out of jail several times and he was able to find some pussy. There's no reason why Gary shouldn't be able to do the same. The only thing that Gary did was sue his parents.

After I finish writing this book, I'm going to create a special web page for Gary and all of the other has-beens that are having a problem getting pussy.

http://www.WHO WANTS/ TO FUCK/ GARY COLEMAN.COM
http://www.WHO WANTS/ TO FUCK/ JIMMY WALKER.COM
http://www.WHO WANTS/ TO FUCK/EMANUEL LEWIS.COM

March On!

The Million Man March was history in the making. Although I didn't attend, it was wonderful to see my black brothers unite together as one. Shortly after the Million Man March, someone came up with the idea of having one for women. They called it the Million Women March. This year I heard that they will be having a Million Family March. I think that the individual planning these marches is really out of touch with the people that really need help.

When I watched both the Million Man and Million Women Marches, I saw individuals that were sure of themselves, individuals that had their shit together. There's no doubt in my mind that the Million Family March will be any different. That's why I think that we should change the direction of theses marches. Instead of having a march for individuals that really don't need atonement, we need to have a march for those that do.

I propose that the next march should be called the Million Crackhead March. These are the assholes that really need to be marching, right? Think of that cousin that stole your wedding ring or that brother or sister that took fifty dollars out of your mother's purse. Were they at the Million Man March? Probably not. Most likely they were robbing your house while you were out at the marches. I know that this sounds a little harsh but think about it. If we can get them all together for one day, that would be one day that we wouldn't have to worry about being robbed. We would also be able to search all of the abandoned buildings and find some of the shit that they stole from us.

A Million Crackhead March. What a wonderful idea.

Lil' Kim Rules!

The war is over. Rap music's sex kitten, Lil' Kim, has won! She has defeated Madonna, Toni Braxton, Jennifer Lopez & Prince. If you're wondering how, just pick up a copy of her new CD. The shit is hot. She's sitting in a limousine…**butt naked!**

I just hope that this isn't a trend. I hope that the guys don't try this. Imagine D'Angelo's black hairy balls or Barry White's fat ass on the cover of a CD.

I'm Wheely Upset

I've had it with these assholes in motorized wheelchairs. They roll around in these miniature buggies thinking that everyone that comes in their path should move out of the way just because they're crippled. They have no respect for pedestrians or motorists. Something needs to be done because they're out of control. One of the bastards rolled over my foot then told me that I should try and be more careful. On another occasion one of them ran into the side of my car. When I got out to see if he was all right, he stuck his middle finger out at me and pealed off. I'm not the only one that has had problems with these crippled fucks. I have friends that feel the same way.

Well, I'm not taking any more shit from these pricks. The next time that I have a run in with one. I'm gonna catch him, tip his chair over and give him a good kick in the ass. Better yet, maybe I'll kidnap one and then roll his ass out onto Interstate 95. Boy, I can see it now...

Peter Jennings: "Hello, viewers, today's top story is about a sick individual out there. He's been terrorizing people in wheelchairs. Can you believe it? As of today there have been five reported cases where individuals in wheelchairs have been tipped over and beaten. The police have no clue as to who it is. The only thing that they do know is that he's black and that he uses the words "Crippled Fuck" after each incident. The police think that this individual is also responsible for crossing out all of the "Wheelchair No Parking Signs" throughout all of the major shopping malls. He has replaced the signs with his own sign which reads:

**'You Can Park Here
These Pricks Don't Deserve Free Parking!'**

A Black Man's Fear

Why is it that black men avoid conversation about their colon? If you mention the word colonoscopy in a room filled with black men, you're liable to get beat down and labeled a fag. This is one test that black men fear that they're going to get a sixty-four on. Now white men, on the other hand, are real anal about taking this test.

<u>Bob's To Do List</u>
Change the oil
Mow the lawn
Go Shopping for food
Get Colonoscopy

I think that it's the definition of the word that scares black men away. The Physicians Medical Reference Dictionary defines the term Colonoscopy as follows:

Colonoscopy: The visual examination of the **INTERIOR** of the **COLON** by means of a **COLONSCOPE.**

106

After reading this, the only way that a black man will get a Colonoscopy is if he's walking down the street and his colon drops out of his ass. And even then, he's gonna somehow try and get out of going to the doctor.

Black Man: "Hey, Leroy....after you finish working on that that transmission, you think you can help me with my colon?"

A Sign

Just the other day I saw a guy in the streets holding a huge parking sign that read:

```
Parking
$15.95
In By 7:00 AM.
Out By 7:00 PM
```

Now don't get me wrong, I'm not knocking the guy's job. Who am I to do that when I write jokes for a living. The person that I have the problem with is his boss. You have to be some kind of asshole to interview someone for a job holding a sign. I can see the arrogant prick right now sitting behind his desk.

Mr. Jenkins: "Hello, Carlos....I see here on your resume that you've held a sign before?"

Carlos: "Yes, Mis tor Jenkins, I old de sign for Elian Gonzalez to stay in de United States and I also old de sign in march to City All with Al Sharpton…No Justice, No Peace. No Justice, No Peace!"

Mr. Jenkins: "Wow, Al Sharpton, huh? How long did you hold that sign for?"

Carlos: "A beady, beady, long dime, Mr. Jenkins. Al Sharpton, he my friend."

Mr Jenkins: "I'm impressed, Carlos. Do you have any references?"

Carlos: "Well, papí…I mean Mr. Jenkins, I old de sign at McDonald and I old de sign at de Burger King."

Mr. Jenkins: "Okay, Carlos, I have four more people to interview. Where can I reach you?"

Carlos: "I now old de sign at de Blimpe on 43rd Street. Ear is de number to de telephone booth on de corner."

Say It Ain't So

I read an article in the Village Voice that claimed that there are some Gangster Thugs out there that might be gay. I don't know about you but this scares the shit out of me. If there's any truth to this then I'm staying inside my house for the rest of my life. The thing that I'm worried about is my inability to handle a situation if it arises.

Gangster Thug: "Yo, yo, what up, nigga?"

Me: "Yo, what's up?"

Gangster Thug: "Yo, that chain on your neck is fly yo. You don't need dat shit right? I mean dat shit would look MAD PHAT on me. What you think?"

Me: "Ahh, well, I sort of just bought it and…"

Gangster Thug: "Man, fuck that! Give me the fucking chain!"

<u>**vs.**</u>

Homo Gangster Thug: "Yo, yo, what up Nigga?"

Me: "Yo, what's up?"

Homo Gangster Thug: "Yo, anybody ever tell you that you have a nice fucking ass?"

Me: "Huh…?"

Homo Gangster Thug: "Yeah, nigga, you heard me. You got a nice ass yo. It's so tight and round. It's like two soccer balls."

Me: "Man, listen I don't want any trouble. Take my chain…Please!"

Homo Gangster Thug: "Nah, nigga, I don't want yo chain. I can't fuck a chain."

Me: "Well then here take my wallet instead."

Homo Gangster Thug: "Man, fuck that shit! Why everybody always got to be thinking that all us gangsta muthafuckas want is jewelry and money? People are always trying to stereotype a muthafucka? Now I done told you what I want. Now RUN THAT ASS NIGGER!"

Me: "Come on man, just take the chain…Please!"

I Can See!

I heard that there's a procedure that Stevie Wonder can get that will restore his vision. The way I see it, there's a good and bad side to this. The good side of course is that Stevie will be able to see for the first time in his life. The bad side is when he takes a look at his hair line all hell's gonna break loose.

Stevie Wonder: "Damn, who the hell has been cornrowing my hair? Ray Charles?"

Never Go Shopping With Your Girlfriend

Never make the mistake of shopping for sexual toys with your girlfriend. I went to a store in New York City called the Pink Pussy Cat. My girlfriend and I decided that we wanted to add a little spice to our sex life. Once in the store, she went her way and I went mine. After about fifteen minutes of browsing, my girlfriend called me over to the front of the store. That's when she pointed down into the showcase and said:

Girlfriend: "This is what I want."

I looked into the glass case and couldn't believe my eyes. It was a vibrator the size of a two liter bottle of Coke. I looked at my girlfriend like she was crazy.

Me: "What the hell are you going to do with that? I hope that you don't think you're gonna put that thing up my ass?"

When the cashier chuckled at what I said, my Girlfriend became very angry.

Girlfriend: "Nigga, this isn't for you. It's for me MISTER SORRY I'M TOO TIRED TONIGHT HONEY."

Me: "Well how the hell do you expect me to make love to you after using that thing? Shit, you probably need a car battery to start it up."

Girlfriend: "I knew that coming here with your immature ass would be a bad idea. You just pick out whatever the hell you think I would like. I'll be outside."

My Girlfriend stormed out of the store leaving me with the task of picking out a vibrator for her. As I looked at them it didn't take me long to find one that I felt was appropriate. I settled on one that was the size of a pen cap. I remember thinking, Yeah, this will do, this looks a lot more like mine.

I'm A Dead Beat Dad

My sons really think that I'm a "Dead Beat Dad." I must admit they're right. Now don't get me wrong, I'm not a Dead Beat Dad in the traditional sense. I'm a dad that misses the beat with respect to Rhythm and Blues music. Every time my boys turn the radio on I fear that they are going to ask me to explain the lyrics. And with the direction that Rhythm and Blues is taking today, this can be very difficult to explain.

Lyrics From R&B Music of Today.

1. I'll kiss the lips below your navel.
2. I want to bust a nut in you.
3. Can I touch you in your private parts.
4. Let me see that thong. (Like the way the booty goes)
5. I'm fucking you tonight.

See what I mean? I can't let them listen to anything that's playing on the radio. When they ride in my car I force them to listen to my pre-recorded tapes.

Dad's Music

1. I'm your boogie man, that's what I am.
2. Keep on truckin baby…. Ya got to keep on… Trucking.
3. Now I am Wonder Mike and I'd like to say hello.
4. Let's dance…Let's dance to the drummer's beat…Let's dance.
5. Last dance…Last chance…For love.

My sons don't even want to ride in the car with me any more. My youngest one, Jamarl, said, "Those are some DEAD BEATS, dad."

Butt Meat

Black men love a woman with a big ass. They can get so creative when describing them. Here is a top ten list of ways to describe a woman's ass.

1. Man, take a look at that rock.
2. Boy, look at that dump truck over there.
3. Check out the onion on her.
4. Damn, her ass is like "Click Cow!"
5. Check out those sweet buns.
6. That's not pudding; that's jelly; No, that's not jelly; that's jam.
7. Man, so what she's ugly. Just walk her in backwards. Then everybody will understand.
8. Her ass is so big; I can rest my lunch tray on it.
9. She has 100% prime beef back there.
10. What a hot rump.

Call Me The Master

My girlfriend caught me masturbating in her bathroom. This had to be one of the most embarrassing situations that I've ever faced. I just don't understand why women get so uptight about this. It's not like I had another woman in her bathroom. It was just me and her Essence Magazine. She made me out to be some kind of pervert. This is how the conversation went after she opened the bathroom door on me.

Her: "What the hell is going on in there?…What are you doing?"

Me: "Huh, what?"

Her: "Nigga, you heard me. It smells like someone is burning rubber in here."

Me: "Honey, will you please close the…"

Her: "Are you jerking off in my house?…I know you're not masturbating in my house?"

Me: "No, I'm not masturbating!"

Her: "Then what are you doing standing here with your pants down and my Essence magazine in your hand?…Shit, you ain't no where near the toilet."

My girlfriend kept pressing me until finally I told her the truth.

121

Me: "Okay, okay...I was masturbating. Are you satisfied now?"

Her: "Well, why in God's name are you doing this? We just made love last night."

Me: "Well, honey, this is something that I like to do by myself sometimes. This is something I do for me."

Her: "Sometimes? How often do you masturbate?"

Me: "Damn, honey, why do you have to say masturbate so loud?"

Her: "What, now your ashamed of the word? If you can funk up my bathroom then you can stand to hear the word masturbate a couple of times. Now answer the question. How often do you do this?"

Me: "That's my business!"

Her: "No, it's not just your business. If we're going to be together, I need to know. I don't want you going over to my mother's house masturbating all over the god damn place."

My girlfriend questioned me for about forty minutes then she told me that I should leave her house and call her when I was done with this "**Perverted Nasty Masturbation Shit!**" I was so mad at her. Once I reached my house, I called her. I had time to think about the situation and I was going to set her straight.

Me: "You're mad at me? Shit, the pizza man masturbates and you let him make you a pie with extra cheese and pepperoni. I don't see you cutting him out of your diet. Think about it, he's smacking the dough with his bare hands—hands that probably just masturbated."

Her: "You know what? You have to be the dumbest man that I've ever dated."

CLICK!

Black Plays

There is an "epidemic" of black plays spreading throughout the United States. I've been to a couple of them and I must admit most of them are entertaining. The problem that I have with these plays are their titles.

1. "Mama I want to Sing....Part 28," Starring the same niggas that stared in part 27, 26, 25 and 24.
2. "God, Please Find Me A Man."
3. "God, Please Forget What I Said. I'll Find My Own man." Starring **Jimmy JJ Walker** from Good Times.
4. "God, We're Running Out Of Has-beens," Starring **Gary Coleman**.
5. God, I'm In Love With My Sister's Man, Starring Sherman Hemsley & Little Richard.

Ice, Ice Baby

I think rapper Ice T should run for political office. Picture him in Washington in and out of meetings striving to help the common man. One thing is for sure, he's gonna keep things real. Imagine him on the floor trying to get a bill passed.

Ice T: "I don't give a fuck how long we have to stay here. I'll filibuster this shit all night long…And if you decide that you're not gonna sign it, I'm prepared to put a cap in your ass. Shit, there are niggas out there that need this shit."

Ice T For President

He'll get my vote that's for sure.

Just Trying To Find A Little Love

I have this secret fantasy that involves African American Female Midgets. I've been infatuated with female midgets since the 80's. Remember midget wrestling? There was this hot little sister that would kick ass! Then wrestling took a nose dive and the only midgets around were the ones in the circus. If you ever tried to date anyone in the circus, you know that this is literally impossible. Everyone is too busy jumping around and acting silly all of the damn time. However, I was able to meet one midget. We dated for a short time but then broke up because she kept begging me to get into one of those teeny weenie cars that they ride around in. I think that she just wanted to show me off to her other midget friends. When I told her this, she punched me really hard in my knee. She really had a short temper. I'm still limping from that shit. Well anyway, I decided to write this piece in an attempt to find another African American Female Midget. They're so hard to find these days.

Just Leave Them Alone

One time while my girlfriend and I were getting dressed I watched her as she reach for her Feminine Deodorant Spray(FDS). When she stepped out of the bathroom, I looked at the bottle and thought, *What the hell? Maybe I should try some of this shit. My balls have been smelling like Jamaican cod fish as of late.* I reached for the bottle and sprayed some all over. Everything was cool until we stepped outside and the air hit my ass. That FDS stuff must trigger from the air because my balls felt like someone had put a blow torch under them. I was screaming and yelling. My girlfriend was yelling back, "Baby, what's wrong, what's wrong?" I couldn't tell her what was wrong. I just ran back upstairs, opened the refrigerator door, pulled out a bottle of Snapple Ice Tea and jammed my balls into it. Now I see why they say that "It's The Best Stuff On Earth." From now on, I'm just gonna leave my balls alone and just let them smell.

10 Reasons Why Female Singing Groups Can't Stay Together

1. Only one of them can sing.

2. Somebody's daddy manages the group.

3. Somebody finds Jesus as their savior and only wants to sing gospel.

4. Somebody's Aunt wants to know, "Why can't my niece sing lead once in a while."

5. The group is number one on the Billboard Charts but still broke.

6. The lead singer gets knocked up but still insists that she can still sing and wear a thong.

7. One member wants to use their fame to save the world instead of making more money.

8. They all get their period at the same time.

9. The leader of the group persuades the members by saying, "Just sign the damn contract. My cousin Bubba looked it over. He said it's fine."

10. The lead singer becomes a selfish bitch and leaves the group to pursue a solo career so she can keep all of the money for herself.

White Man's Fear

It really sucks being white and bald. It wouldn't be so bad if there were some cool bald headed white guys to look up to. Black men can emulate R&B singers and practically the entire NBA. White guys have no one. The last cool bald white guy was Kojak and he's been dead for years. So now when white men step into a crowded room they have to deal with comments like, "Hey, Tommy, how's the chemotherapy going dude? Well, don't worry. You still have your eyebrows, bro" or "Hey, Tommy, are you losing the hair on your ass also?"

Flying

White airplane pilots have too much pride. I heard an audio tape between a white pilot and a white air traffic controller and you wouldn't even know that a plane was about to crash.

Control Center: "Control to Flight 802, our radar indicates that you're approaching Kennedy Airport twenty minutes before schedule. Is everything okay up there? Over."

Pilot: "Ahh yes, everything is okay Control. However, we are experiencing a little problem with our descent...Ladies and Gentlemen, please return to your seat and put your seat belts on."

Control Center: "Command to Flight 802, it looks like your wing is on fire! Over!"

Pilot: "Ahh yes, Command, I noticed that...Ladies and Gentlemen, in the event of smoke or fire, your oxygen masks are located in the red panel above your head."

Control Center: "Flight 802 you're about to splashdown into the Hudson! Do you read? Over!"

Pilot: "Yes, Command. Ladies and Gentlemen for the next few minutes we will be experiencing a bit of turbulence, no need to..."

That's why I'll fly with a black pilot over a white one any day of the week. A black pilot will keep it real!

Control Center: "Yo, Bubba, is everything okay up there. Over!"

Black Pilot: "Over? Over is what it is. This shit here is about to blow the fuck up! It's smoking something terrible up here. Listen, Command, y'all hold on for a taste…Ladies and Gentlemen, this is Captain Bubba. Yo, in a little while you're gonna feel some turbulence like you never felt before. So fuck the seat belts, the oxygen masks and all of that other emergency bullshit that we talked about at the beginning of the flight. Now I'm gonna keep it real. The flight panel is fucked up; it looks like Chinese. There's so much smoke in the cockpit that I can't see my dick. In short, our asses is dead. I suggest that you do what I'm about to do. Grab a stewardess and fuck her in the ass. Over!"

Ghetto Heaven

Here is a short list that we've compiled for those of you who are not sure about what being "Ghetto" really is.

1. Anyone who puts his or her telephone bill in their unborn child's name is Ghetto.

2. Anyone who brings their own hot sauce to a restaurant is Ghetto.

3. When people mistake your yellow teeth for gold plated teeth, you're Ghetto.

4. When your hair is black and you put a blond weave in, you're Ghetto.

5. When you're at church and you reach into the collection plate and make change for a dollar, fake that you put money in or steal change from the collection plate, then put it in an envelope with your name on it and place it back into the collection plate, you're fucked up and Ghetto.

6. If you replace your broken car or television antenna with a hanger, you're Ghetto.

7. Anyone who wears silver, gold or bronze hair is Ghetto.

8. Buying roses for your girlfriend from the guy standing in the middle of the street holding a white bucket is Ghetto.

9. Farting and leaving the room is not only Ghetto but nasty also.

10. When you own a Mercedes, Lexus, BMW or Porsche and still live in the projects, you're Ghetto.

11. Women that think that arm pit hair is sexy are Ghetto.

12. Women with more hair on their legs then they have on their head are Ghetto.

Reach Out And Touch

The black church is making an effort to reach out to the youth of today. They have become more liberal with their policies concerning music and dress attire. Though I do enjoy some of the new gospel music that's out, I think that the dress attire should remain conservative. I was at a church in Harlem and this girl walked into the church with a halter top and a mini skirt on. When she went to the altar to give thanks, I ended up giving thanks too because she had a thong on. I've joined about five churches in the last two month. This is better than porno. Last week while I was going through my usual prayer, for some reason, this is what came out,

Me: "God bless my mother. God bless my father. God bless my sister. And God bless my brother.... Amen......Oh yeah one more thing, God bless that sister that's wearing the purple poodle printed panties. God damn she has a nice ass...Amen."

This just isn't right. Maybe we should forget about liberalizing the black church and go back to the boring, empty, rhythmless, conservative church. If we don't, I'm sure that there's someone out there looking to take things even a step further.

Announcer: "Brothers and sisters, today's guess speaker comes to us all the way from Los Angeles California. He's a former gang member, ex-con, child molester, wife beater and recovering alcoholic. He's here today to give us some words of inspiration. Put your hand's together for the one… and only…..Bishop Big Balls Johnson…Come on, show your love for Bishop Big Balls."

Bishop Big Balls: "Can I get an Amen up in dis muthafucka?"

Congregation: "Amen."

Bishop Big Balls: "Y'all niggas act like somebody done smoked your homey up in here. Now can I get a muthafucking Amen up in here? Say it like you mean it!"

Congregation: "AMEN!"

Bishop Big Balls: "Alright, alright…I'd like to welcome you all to the church where anything goes. Ya feel like screaming out and saying muthafucka, feel free. If you want to pick your nose and put your boggers under the pews, go for it, because your in the church where anything goes. Now your Pastor has brought some disturbing news to me. He said that last week he asked the congregation for an offering to fix the church piano, said that it needs to be tuned up. Now when the final count was made for this collection it came to sixty-six dollars and seventy-three cents. Now what the fuck do you expect your pastor to do with this kind of money? Shit, it cost ninety-five dollars to get the nigger to come out and just look at the shit. Y'all is a bunch of cheap ass muthafuckas up in here. God says to give but all I see is a bunch of playa hatin' cheap ass muthafuckas up in here. Y'all have to understand that if you give, you get! God will make sure of that. God's not gonna jerk you. God pays his bills. He ain't like us; he's never late. Think about it, How are we gonna worship a God with fucked up credit. God's TRW report is alllllllll that and a bag of chips. So in closing, I'd just like to let y'all know that if you give a little, you'll get a little. But if ya give your all....Y'all know Sister Pearl right?... Well, Sister Pearl came over to my trailer last night and gave me her all. Sister Pearl, stand up so that the congregation can take a look at you. Ya see that hat that Sister Pearl is wearing, the one with all those plastic grapes and fruit and shit on it? Sister Pearl got that hat because she gave it up! She gave it alllllll up for God! Sister Pearl told me that she's been giving it up all of her life and she's living well because of it. She has a double wide trailer with a water bed in it. God is good!"

My Baby Boy

My oldest son David is handsome. He's everything that I wanted to be as a kid. He has clear skin, the option to wear his hair long or short and at the age of twelve, he's six feet and a solid 155 lbs. In Short, he's a twelve year old hunk. I'm starting to notice that the little girls his age are starting to look at him a little differently, and my son doesn't have a clue. These days a girl that is twelve years old has a mind of an eighteen year old. These little girls are smart; they're like little miniature women.

David Jr: "Hey Tawanda, you want to trade Pokémon cards with me?"

Tawanda: "Sure David but it's too cold to play outside. Lets go to your room."

David Jr: "Okay, swell…"

After twenty minutes of trading

Tawanda: "David, I'm tired of trading cards. I have a new game that I want to play."

David Jr: "A new game? Alright, let's play. What is the game called?"

Tawanda: "It's called *"Poke—me—mon"*

David Jr: "*Poke-me-mon?* I never heard of this game. How do you play? How many cards do we need?"

Tawanda: "We don't need any cards, silly. You have what we need right there."

David Jr: "Right there? Right where?"

Tawanda: "Right there behind your zipper."

David Jr: "Noooo, no, we can't play with that! My Dad said that it's strictly for urinating only."

Tawanda: "Well, it's no wonder your mom left him."

David Jr: "What? What are you talking about, what's that got to do with it?"

Tawanda: "Never mind. Just take it out and start poking me with it. Sort of like when we used to play the *Battle Sword Commando* game but instead of swinging your sword from side to side, your gonna push it in and out, okay?"

David Jr: "Okay, but my dad said….."

Tawanda: "Oh, the hell with your dad. After we finish playing you'll be able to teach your dad a thing or two and maybe he can get you a new mother and keep this one happy."

David Jr: "Heeeeeeeey, this game is all right. I can't wait to teach my little brother."

Tawanda: "NOOOOOOOOOOOO! NO! You can't play this game with your brother! You'll go to jail for a million trillion years. You play this game with me and only me, you understand?"

David Jr: "Okay, Tawanda, okay, dag! Are we finish playing yet?"

Tawanda: "Just shut up and keep on playing, you'll know when it's over. That is the best part of the game."

Eye Of The Tiger

White people love Tiger Woods. I love him too but my love is nothing compared to the way white people love him. Tiger could be walking down a busy city street and white people will stop what they're doing and start clapping. They don't say, "Hi". They don't say, "Nice to meet you." They just clap. Anytime you can make white people clap for you, you're in there! Because white people just don't clap for any old nigger. You have to be special. And when Tiger told the world that he's not black, it was like putting vanilla icing on a chocolate cake. Tiger is so well loved that he even had white people testifying that he's not black.

Arnold Palmer: "No, no, Tiger's not black, You try playing golf all day at Pebble Beach for four hours. You'll be as black as that nigger from "Roots" Kon-ta Kenta.

I got fed up with all of the controversy about his ethnicity. I decided to take a poll. The individuals that participated in this poll are experts on who is black. Below is an interview with their head representative, Mr. Mellio.

Me: "Hello, Mr. Mellio. Can you state your occupation?"

Mr. Mellio: "Ah, yes, I am the president of the NYC Taxi and Limousine Commission."

Me: "Okay, well let me get right to it. You know Tiger Woods don't you?"

Mr. Mellio starts clapping his hands.

Me: "Mr. Mellio, could you stop clapping and answer the question?"

Mr. Mellio: "Oh, sorry. Every time I hear his name, I can't help my self. Yes, I know him."

Me: "Well, here's the question. Would you or any of your driver's pick Tiger Woods up and take him to Harlem?"

Mr. Mellio: "Are you fucking crazy! Hell no! We wouldn't take that nigger to Manhattan! He's a good golf player but that shit doesn't mean anything when you're in Harlem at night. We didn't pick-up Danny Glover's black ass, and we wouldn't pick Tiger up either. What a stupid question...Hey, do you think you can get me some tickets to his next match?"

It's Official, Tiger is Black!

Puerto Rican Day Parade

I'm glad that my girlfriend and I decided to take a taxi home after the Puerto Rican Day Parade. I saw the unruly bunch of drunken psychos' on the news and I don't know if my relationship with my girlfriend would have been able to survive something like that. Women expect you to rescue them like a knight in shining armor. They don't want to hear excuses of any kind, regardless of the circumstances.

Me: "Baby, there were fifteen men holding me down. I couldn't break loose."

Women want you to put on your cape and rescue them by any means necessary. So believe me when I say that if the mob would have grabbed my woman, I would have ended the relationship the very next day because I know what the next date would be like.

Me: "Honey, wasn't that movie great? I think he should definately get an Oscar. What do you think?"

Her: "Yeah, he sure was good…I wish that "Shaft" was there with us that day after the Puerto Rican Day Parade. He would have shot all of those assholes in their dicks and crushed their balls with his bare hands. He probably would have had time to save your punk ass too. One thing is for sure, Shaft wouldn't have any lame ass excuses!"

Glossary

ASSHOLE: PERSON THAT OWES YOU MONEY AND WON'T PAY IT BACK. PERSON THAT CUTS YOU OFF ON HIGHWAY. YOUR STEP FATHER.

BUBBA: BLACK MAN'S NAME.

CLEOPHUS: ANOTHER BLACK MAN'S NAME.

DICK: TOOL USED BY MEN. IF TOOL IS USED INCORRECTLY COULD CAUSE ARGUMENT, FIST FIGHTS AND EVENTUALLY DIVORCE.

HOMOSEXUAL: 1. TWO MEN ENGAGED IN SEX. 2. THAT FRIEND THAT ACOMPANIES YOUR SON EVERY YEAR FOR THANKSGIVING AND CHRISMAS DINNER.

I'S: TERM USED BY SLAVES AND GED RECIPIENTS. **EXAMPLE:** I'S GO AND FIX THE SHED NOW. I'S GONNA CRUSH UP THIS GLASS AND PUT IT IN MASTER'S CORNMEAL. I'S REALLY NEED THIS JOB.

JACKASS BALLS: I HAVE NO IDEA WHAT THIS MEANS. I SAW IT IN THE BOOK *THE INVISIBLE MAN*.

NIGGER: TERM COMMONLY USED BY WHITE PEOPLE BEFORE AND DURING THE CIVIL RIGHTS MOVEMENT. (PLEASE NOTE: IF TERM IS USED NOW BY WHITE PERSON, WHITE PERSON COULD END UP IN HOSPITAL) HOWEVER, WORD CAN BE USED BY BLACK PEOPLE TO GREET AND SHOW LOVE TOWARDS EACH OTHER. SEE MULTIPLE WAYS TO USE BELOW.

NIGGER: WHITE PEOPLE USE THIS ONE.

NIGGAS: RAPPERS AND BLACK PEOPLE USE THIS ONE (WHITE RAPPERS CAN ALSO US THIS ONE.)

PUSSY: DEVICE USED TO GET:

1. MONEY
2. POWER
3. MARRIED OR DIVORCED
4. THE RENT PAID
5. A NEW RING OR BRACELET
6. YOUR BEST FRIEND'S MAN
7. PUT IN JAIL
8. THE CON ED BILL PAID
9. THAT JOB THAT YOU DON'T DESERVE
10. A DATE WITH THE PRESIDENT OF THE UNITED STATES.

TITTIES: DEVICES USED TO GET THE SAME THINGS THAT PUSSY WILL GET YOU. (PLEASE NOTE THAT TITTIES MUST BE A "D" CUP.)

WHITEY: TERM USED BY BLACK PEOPLE TO DESCRIBE CAUCASION PEOPLE. TERM USED BEFORE, DURING AND AFTER THE CIVIL RIGHTS MOVEMENT. TERM USED BY BLACK MEN IN HEATED DISCUSSION FOR REASONS WHY THEY CAN'T FIND, LOOK, OR KEEP A JOB.

About the Author

David Asbery made his literary debut as co-author of the Black Board Best seller, "BOOTLEG," by Damon Wayans (Publisher Harper Collins). Born in Manhattan, David now resides in Queens where he is working on a new book entitled "Single Dad...Not Singled Out!"

David Asbery

Seymour Swan has appeared at numerous comedy clubs nationwide. With a stellar eleven year career in stand-up comedy, he now has a weekly show on Friday and Saturday nights at the New York Comedy Club.

About the Illustrator

Frank Page was born with a pencil in his hand which really ticked off his mother. He graduated from Cazenovia College in 1997 with a BFA in Illustration. He has been published in Children and Families and the Artist's Magazine. See what else he can do by going to his web site. http://www.frankpage.net.

Notes

To obtain a copy of *Bootleg* or to get ticket information to see Seymour live, send your email to *www.omasberry.com* or write to Omas & Berry Publications P.O. Box 1594 Grand Central Station New York, NY 10163.